TEAMWORK Isn't My Thing, and I Don't Like to SHARE!

To Graf
Love, Julia

Written by
Julia Cook

Illustrated by
Kelsey De Weerd

BOYS TOWN Press
Boys Town, Nebraska

Teamwork Isn't My Thing, and I Don't Like to Share!

ISBN 978-1-934490-35-8

Published by the Boys Town Press
13603 Flanagan Blvd.
Boys Town, NE 68010

For a Boys Town Press catalog, call **1-800-282-6657**
or visit our website: **BoysTownPress.org**

Publisher's Cataloging-in-Publication Data

Cook, Julia, 1964-

Teamwork isn't my thing, and I don't like to share! / written by Julia Cook ; illustrated by Kelsey De Weerd. -- Boys Town, NE : Boys Town Press, c2012.

p. ; cm.
(Best me I can be ; 4th)

ISBN: 978-1-934490-35-8

Audience: grades K-6.
Summary: RJ is having another bad day ... but with the help of his coach, RJ learns that working as a team and sharing are skills needed not just on the soccer field, but in school and at home too.

1. Children--Life skills guides--Juvenile fiction. 2. Teamwork (Sports)--Juvenile fiction. 3. Cooperativeness--Juvenile fiction. 4. Cooperation--Juvenile fiction. 5. Sharing in children--Juvenile fiction. 6. Interpersonal relations in children--Juvenile fiction. 7. [Success--Fiction. 8. Teamwork (Sports)--Fiction. 9. Cooperativeness--Fiction. 10. Sharing--Fiction. 11. Interpersonal relations--Fiction.] I. De Weerd, Kelsey. II. Series: Best me I can be (Boys Town) ; no. 4.

PZ7.C76984 T43 2012

E 1207

Printed in the United States
10 9 8 7 6

Boys Town Press is the publishing division of Boys Town, a national organization serving children and families.

My name is RJ. People say that I need to be more of a team player and learn how to share. The truth is - I already am a team player. I play on a soccer team and we have at least two games a week. As far as sharing goes, it's just not my favorite thing to do.

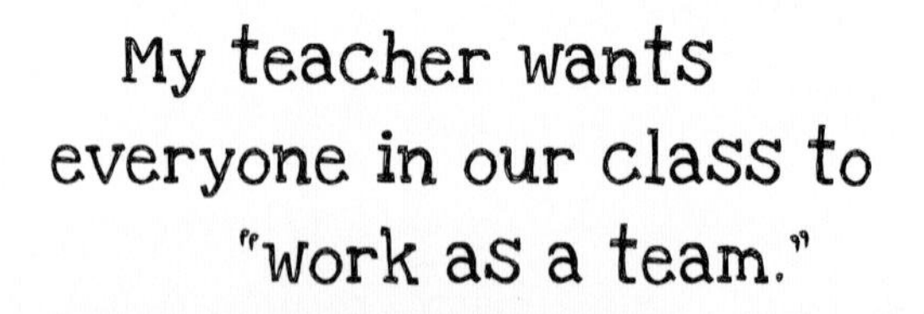

My teacher wants everyone in our class to "work as a team."

She says that TEAM stands for

Together

Everyone

Achieves

More!

Actually, I think it stands for

Together

Everybody

Acts

MEAN!

A few days ago, she broke us up into teams of four and assigned each group a project. My team's project was to do research on mummies, make a poster, and give a presentation to our class.

I got stuck with Bossy Bernice, who thinks she knows everything, Frankie the new kid, who still scribbles, and Norma. She picks her nose ... and then she eats it!

We made a plan to use toilet paper
to wrap one of us up like a mummy.
Everyone wanted to be the mummy ... even me.

Bernice yelled at us because
nobody would do what she said.

Frankie cried when
we wouldn't let him make the poster.

And Norma picked her
nose the whole time
and then she called
the rest of us names.

"I don't want to be on a team,"
I said to my teacher.
"I just want to work by myself!"

"RJ," she said, "when you work well with others, you can get so much more done! Besides, you need to learn to share responsibilities."

I don't like to share either,
I thought to myself.

Yesterday, when I got home from school,
I headed straight for the cookie jar.
The jar had only one cookie in it.

I grabbed the cookie
and was about to take a bite
when I heard my mom say,
"RJ! Please share that last cookie with
your sister. Break it in half."

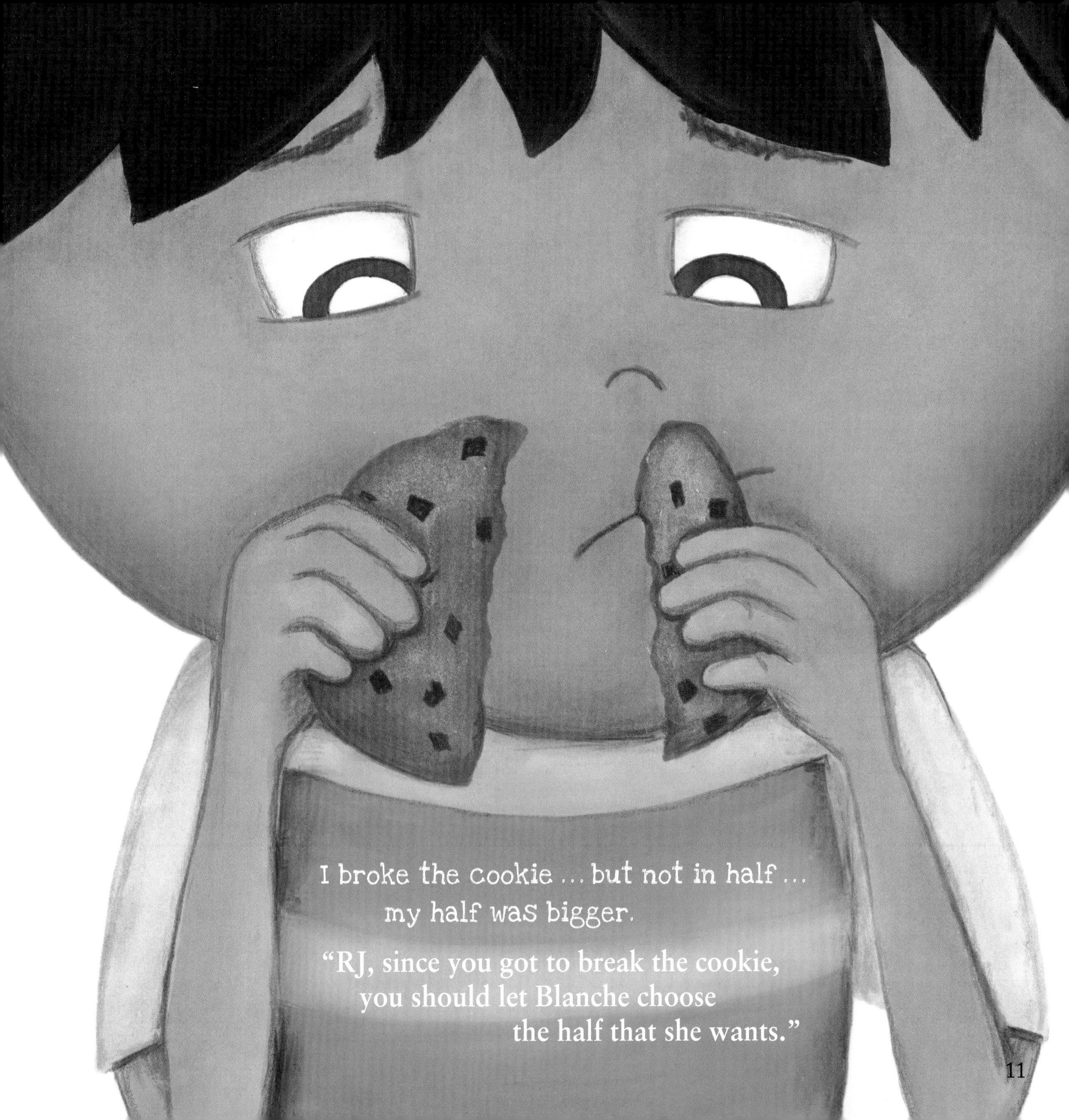

I broke the cookie ... but not in half ...
my half was bigger.

"RJ, since you got to break the cookie,
you should let Blanche choose
the half that she wants."

"Yeah, if I broke the cookie, RJ,
I would give you first choice."

"And I would have left
you with the small piece.

Be happy, that's the
one you ended up with."

“RJ!” my mom said, “that’s not how sharing works.”

My mom made me give Blanche part of my half. She ended up getting more cookie than I did!

That night after soccer practice,
I told my coach about my terrible week.

"I hate to be in a group
and work as a team.

The kids get all mad
and act really mean.

I'd rather just do the
work by myself.

I really don't feel like
I need any help.

And then I get home, and my Mom tells me to share
the very last cookie, 'cause the cookie jar's bare.

She gets all mad 'cause
I don't do it right,

and I end up with a half
that has three less bites!"

"RJ," my coach said, "your teacher is right!
Together, everyone does achieve more!"

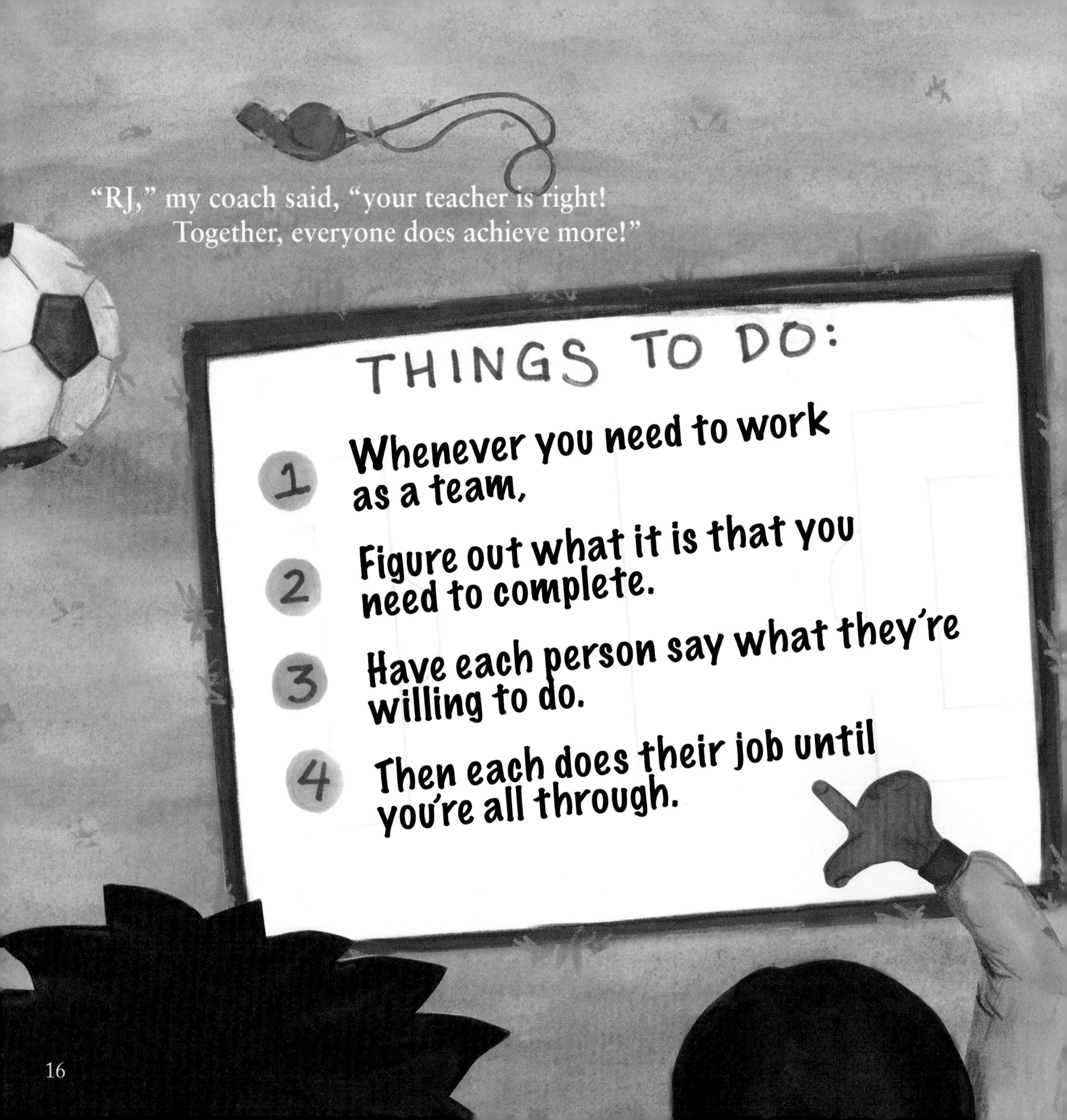

THINGS TO DO:

1. Whenever you need to work as a team,
2. Figure out what it is that you need to complete.
3. Have each person say what they're willing to do.
4. Then each does their job until you're all through.

"RJ, could you be on this soccer team
all by yourself and win any games?"

"No, that would be impossible," I said.

"Well, your school project is just like a soccer game,
and the kids in your group are just like your teammates.
Each person on this team has skills. For example,
Sam is one of the best goalies in the league, but could he play forward?"

"No," I said. "He's as slow as a snail."

"No one can be good at everything,
but everyone is good at something.
The best part about working together is that
each person can use his strengths to help the team.

RJ, you are a great team member on the soccer
field, now do the same thing in your classroom.
With everyone helping, you'll finish faster, and
each of you won't have to work as hard."

"As far as sharing is concerned,
you'll find that your life will be much better if you share.
People who are good at sharing end up being happier than those who don't.
And when you share, others will want to share with you."

When you see something
that needs to be shared:

Let others go first,
you need to be fair.

Be kind and be patient,
then ask for a turn.

When you're finished,
give it back.

Sharing's easy to learn.

"RJ, you are great at sharing
the ball on the field with your teammates,
now do the same thing off the field.

Besides, not only can you share the good stuff,
you can also share the work – like when you
have to do a class project about mummies!"

As I walked home from soccer practice,
I thought about everything my coach had told me.
What he said really did make sense.

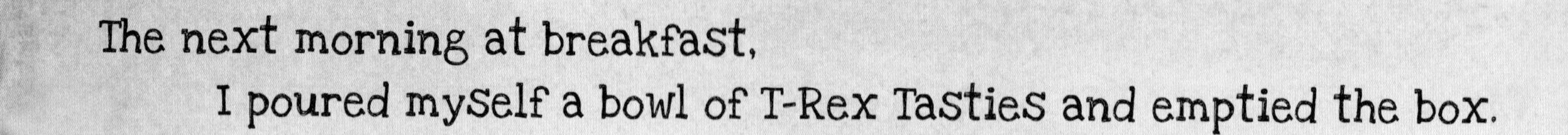

The next morning at breakfast,
I poured myself a bowl of T-Rex Tasties and emptied the box.

"Hey," said Blanche,
"I want some of those too!"

I felt like saying
"No, I had them first!"
But instead, I poured part of
them into her bowl.
My pour wasn't even and
she ended up getting more than me.

She gave me her bowl and said,

"Thanks for sharing, RJ.
Here, you can have the big one."

That day at school when my group
worked on the mummy project,
I told them what my coach
had said about teamwork.
We all decided to start over.

Everybody picked a job that they could do well.

Bernice made a list of what all of us were doing and we let her be the supervisor.

She gave us each a topic to research.

We all collected information and then shared what we had learned with the group.

I wrote out the poster
lightly in pencil, and
Frankie traced over
my letters in marker
so that he didn't scribble.

We decided to let Norma be the mummy.
(Maybe if we wrap her entire body up in tissue,
she'll figure out how to blow her nose with it!)

Sometimes, I still like to work by myself,
But working with others can bring lots of help.
When we all work together, we get so much done!
And not only that, we have a whole lot more fun!

Sharing's not easy. Sometimes it's hard.

But it makes me a better friend and will help me go far.

Sharing with others will show them I care.

My life's gotten better now that I share!

Tips for Parents and Educators

WORKING AS A TEAM

- Encourage the concept of "teamwork" early. Work together to pick up toys; cook together and clean up the mess; wash the car as a team, etc. Show your child at an early age that working as a team can be fun and often is much easier than working alone.
- Remind your child that "everyone is good at something, but nobody can be good at everything." Working as a team allows people to use their individual strengths to contribute to the whole cause.
- Being a part of a team helps children develop better social interaction, collaboration, and communication skills. Give children the opportunity to become part of a team by involving them in team sports, volunteer activities, music or dance lessons – anything that will encourage working cooperatively with others.
- Good teammates must be able to do three things well: listen to others without interrupting, communicate with the members of the team and share ideas, and have confidence both in themselves and in the team as a whole.
- Team kids up to do tasks around the house or in the classroom. Develop a reward system that recognizes team effort and success.

SHARING

- The concept of sharing may not yet have developed in children under the age of two, but model the skill early by taking turns, sharing a toy or food with them.
- Set a good example for your child. You are your child's coping instructor! Role-play sharing and couple the experiences with enjoyment and praise.
- Call positive attention to the benefits of sharing by pointing out examples in your home, the environment, or school whenever you can (for example, mama bird sharing food with her babies, sharing the remote for the TV, sharing the care of a classroom pet).
- Don't make a child share everything. Some items can be "special" and should not have to be shared. Put those items away while others are around so that they don't cause contention.
- If your child has a difficult time sharing and is over the age of four, offer an incentive (a tangible reward) for making an effort to share. To become good at sharing, a child must "believe" that sharing is in his or her best interest.

For more parenting information, visit boystown.org/parenting.

Boys Town Press Books by Julia Cook

Kid-friendly books to teach social skills

Reinforce the social skills RJ learns in each book by ordering its corresponding teacher's activity guide and skill posters.

978-1-934490-20-4
978-1-934490-21-1 (AUDIO BOOK)
978-1-934490-34-1 (SPANISH)
978-1-934490-23-5 (ACTIVITY GUIDE)

978-1-934490-25-9
978-1-934490-26-6 (AUDIO BOOK)
978-1-934490-53-2 (SPANISH)
978-1-934490-27-3 (ACTIVITY GUIDE)

978-1-934490-28-0
978-1-934490-29-7 (AUDIO BOOK)
978-1-934490-32-7 (ACTIVITY GUIDE)

978-1-934490-35-8
978-1-934490-36-5 (AUDIO BOOK)
978-1-934490-37-2 (ACTIVITY GUIDE)

978-1-934490-43-3
978-1-934490-44-0 (AUDIO BOOK)
978-1-934490-45-7 (ACTIVITY GUIDE)

978-1-934490-49-5
978-1-934490-50-1 (AUDIO BOOK)
978-1-934490-51-8 (ACTIVITY GUIDE)

978-1-934490-67-9
978-1-934490-68-6 (AUDIO BOOK)
978-1-934490-69-3 (ACTIVITY GUIDE)

NEW TITLES

A book series to help kids get along.

Making Friends is An Art!
Cliques Just Don't Make Cents
Tease Monster
Peer Pressure Gauge
Hygiene...You Stink!
I Want to Be the Only Dog
The Judgmental Flower
Table Talk
Rumor Has It...

A book series to help kids master the art of communicating.

Well, I Can Top That!
Decibella
Gas Happens
Technology Tail

A book series to help kids take responsibility for their behavior.

But It's Not My Fault
Baditude
The Procrastinator
Cheaters Never Prosper
That Rule Doesn't Apply to Me

BoysTownPress.org

For information on Boys Town, its Education Model®, Common Sense Parenting®, and training programs:
boystowntraining.org | boystown.org/parenting
training@BoysTown.org | 1-800-545-5771

For parenting and educational books and other resources:
BoysTownPress.org
btpress@BoysTown.org | 1-800-282-6657